I would like to dedicate my book to the memory of my wonderful wife Ann (Annie).

LIFE AND LOVE

LIFE AND LOVE

Alan Lewis

First paperback edition

978-1-80541-408-7 (paperback)
978-1-80541-465-0 (hardback)
978-1-80541-409-4 (eBook)

CHAPTER 1

He was lying on his back on a wooden plank, naked except for his pants. Straddling the lower part of his body was a figure dressed all in black wearing a hood. The figure had no face. Over the figure's shoulder he could see another figure, a young face, raised arm pointing towards him, screaming, "That's him!" The figure straddling him raised a knife high in front of him and with both hands plunged the weapon down towards his chest.

Steve rose up shuddering, no not again: the same dream, nightmare, that had plagued him time and time again since he had been imprisoned. Beads of sweat ran down his face from his forehead. He stood up from the chair where he had fallen asleep, took a handkerchief from the pocket of his jeans, and dried off his face. The door to the room opened. "OK, it's all completed they have everything they need, you can leave," said a voice belonging to a detective he only knew as Len. "Got everything?" Steve picked up his nearly empty holdall from the floor and glanced around the room. What else was he expected to have other than what he was wearing, after spending four years in prison, four years for a murder he did not commit. He followed the officer along a corridor, through to a large open office where several other officers were at work. No one looked towards him. Steve thought, 'They probably still think I'm guilty or at least involved in the murder of the girl Jackie, and have no idea why I've been kept at the police station for the last few days'. Well, it did not matter what they thought. The judges, with all the new evidence presented at his appeal, had overturned his conviction and ordered his release.

He walked down the steps at the front of the police station and stood at the bottom, looking up at the cloudy sky. The ground was wet following a brief shower and there was that damp earth smell in the air. It was 1st June – not a great start to so-called Flaming June. He took a thin casual jacket from his holdall and slipped it on, being careful not to drop the envelope containing the manuscript for the beginning of a book he had started to write whilst in prison. Without a glance behind him he strode off towards the railway station. He was going home. All traces of the limp he had as a result of the injuries he suffered when serving in Afghanistan were gone. The only good thing from being imprisoned was the treatment he received on his injured leg. Several operations to removed fragments of bullets had been successful. At the station he boarded the train travelling to Brandon Junction, a two hour 40 minute journey, where he could get a connection for the short trip to his home village of Sweetwater. Midmorning, the rush hour firmly over, the train had few passengers. He took a window seat, placing his holdall on the seat next to him to deter any company. He just wanted to be alone with time to think. The train moved off, his head against the window, and he thought about how the hell everything in his life had gone so wrong.

He thought of his childhood, living with his loving parents and younger brother Martin in the small cottage at the end of a row of houses in Sweetwater. A smile lit up his face that quickly turned into a grimace as a picture of Martin flashed across his mind, saddened by memory of the fun that two brothers had when growing up together. Yes, they had fights, nothing serious just over silly arguments so soon forgotten. The fun they had sitting on the plank that crossed the river Swee at the rear of their property. Their dad had placed the plank there having rescued it from the timber yard where he worked. What a plank. Solid oak, twelve feet long, a foot wide and at least two inches thick. Now people could cross the river and take a short route across the field to the village, instead of following the road which took a long curve over the old stone bridge to where it joined up with the village main street. The brothers would sit on the plank dangling their legs over the side, fishing with the home-made rods their dad had made, each hoping to catch a whopper but so happy and excited to catch a small perch, roach or even a dace, laughing as they returned a fish back into the river and then tried to catch it again. Martin now dead, drowned in the river having fallen off the plank, when Steve should have been there to save him. At 16, two years older than Martin, he and his brother both attended the local school and would walk there and back together over the river via the plank, but on that fateful day they had one of their silly arguments. Steve had wanted to watch his best friend John play football for the school and Martin had wanted to get home to watch something on TV, so with Martin promising to go home via the road and not to use the short cut across the field, he had let him go home by himself. After the football had finished he had made

4

his way home. He would never be able to forget that homecoming, seeing a police vehicle outside the cottage. When he entered both his parents were in tears, hugging one another in obvious grief. A witness had seen Martin jumping up on down on the plank before slipping and falling into the river. Although the witness had rescued him from the water, he was unable to revive him.

After that things were never the same for him at home. His mother never once blamed him in any way for the tragedy, but his father did. He clearly remembered his father saying to him after the funeral, "It was your duty to look after your brother. You failed him, and you failed us." His relationship with his father had never been the same again, and when he left school he remembered the argument with his father about going to work in the garage owned by the Tune Brothers instead of a job at the timber yard.

The click-click of the rails lulled him into sleep until he was roused by the train lurching to a stop. Looking out of the window he saw several workmen in yellow jackets moving about outside, obviously doing track repairs. He looked beyond the men at the green fields, hedges and trees swaying in the light breeze, some still showing traces of blossom. He had forgotten how beautiful the countryside looked at this time of the year. The train remained stationary for a few minutes before moving off. Memories flooded back. Things had started well at the garage now owned by the three bothers: Jake the eldest, and Raymond a few years younger; then there was the third and youngest brother, James. He had thought of James many times in prison, recollecting how it was explained to him about his condition. His mother had him very late in her life, some 20 years after Ray, a mistake, unwanted pregnancy, whatever. When James' mother was giving birth serious problems arose resulting in James being starved of oxygen leaving him with permanent brain damage. The brothers' father had retired and Jake was now running the business. Would he still have a job there? If he asked? Did he want to work there? And of course there was Julie.

The train entered a tunnel the clicking of the tracks being replaced by a shuddering on the windows, then back out into countryside and the resuming of the click-click of the rails. Julie – teenage lovers so long ago. He smiled to himself and even chuckled as he remember their first attempt at sex, him as they lay semi-naked on the bank of the river behind his home, attempting for the first time to unroll a condom which Julie had stolen from her brother's wallet. He had it the wrong way round and it would not unroll, then it pinged off and he had to frantically search for it in the long grass, while all the time she was giggling. At last he found and fitted it and then they had sex, the first time for both of them.

Life had been pretty good over the next months; he enjoyed working at the garage and building up a friendly relationship with the younger brother James. Then it had all changed. They were caught red-handed by Julie's older brother Carl while they were having sex in the back of one of her father's used cars. He was dragged from the car and punched by Carl several times in his face and body while he screamed, "You come near her again and I will fucking kill you!" Leaving him lying on the ground struggling for breath, he saw Julie being dragged away.

It did not end there. The next day at work Carl came storming into the garage and spoke to Jake and Ray in the office while pointing at him through the office window. Carl left, shaking his fist at him as he did so. He had then been called into the office and sacked. How angry he had felt then.

Carl and Julie's family owned several car showrooms throughout the county with a BMW dealership. Any cars they took in part exchange were examined, serviced at Tune's before being displayed at one of the showrooms and offered for sale. Carl had made it perfectly clear to the Tune brothers that this arrangement would cease if they did not get rid of Steve. He remembered collecting his personal stuff and as he left the garage, ruffling James hair. He was surprised when James jumped from his chair to give him a huge lingering hug.

Steve wondered what had happen to James while he had been imprisoned. He had been living with Jake and his family, attending the community centre in Kenton, a town 13 miles from Sweetwater, three days a week. On his free days he helped doing odd jobs around the garage, sweeping up, running errands, or just sitting on a chair outside the garage office whittling away on pieces of wood with an old small bone-handle sheath knife attempting to make tent pegs, something the community teachers had given him to do. Was he still there or had he been placed in some institution: something Ray was always threatening to get Jake to do.

On returning home that day, he had to explain to his father, who surprisingly was not unhappy that he had left the garage, although he had not told him the real reason for his dismissal, just saying that work was scarce and they could not afford to employ him any longer. His father got him a job at the timber yard working alongside his mate and best friend John. This work was boring: mostly loading or unloading trucks and stacking timber. During lunch time breaks they would play football with some of the other workmen on the spare ground behind the yard where John would show off his skills. He had been signed on by Kenton Town FC and hoped that would lead to better prospects. Steve would go to watch him on Saturdays when they played at home. There was no doubt John was a very talented player but he knew there were many other players of the same ability and it was a matter of luck if you were spotted by a football scout and made it to a professional level.

CHAPTER 2

Life was challenging, but seeing Julie without her brother knowing did help break the monotony. Friday nights at The Raven, the local pub/restaurant where they would play darts, was the highlight of the week. For once he was better than John in at least one sport. It was at one of these nights that John had told him of his intention to join the army and hopefully see something of the world. He could still picture the look on John's face when he said he would join him. The look of anguish on his mother's face when he told his parents of his intention to join up. His mum was so worried he might end up involved in some other country's war, while his father just said, "Might make a man of you, just remember to keep your head down." He smiled as he recalled this advice, as it was something he had forgotten to do.

The train rattled into Brandon Junction and he alighted to await his connection to Sweetwater. He longed for a drink but decided as it was only a twenty minute journey he could wait until he reached home.

His train arrived and again was fairly empty, and as he sat by the window, he anticipated that this was going to be a different welcome home from the last time he made this journey, returning home after leaving the army, a so-called hero. Those years in the army were some of the happiest times he could remember since the tragic death of his brother. Yes, he had seen some of the world. Visited some amazing countries on joint manoeuvres and special training courses. The training had been hard. He thought on several occasions he had made the biggest mistake of his life in enlisting, but things did get better, probably due to Sergeant Bass. A man whose life he had later saved, and whose letters he still received, helping to make life bearable during his time in prison. Sergeant Bass. God, how he once hated that man with his constant urging, goading, and at times even bullying, to do better at whatever exercise they were engaged in. John, however, took to the army like a duck to water. His football skills made him a regular and popular player in the army team, where they had won matches against the other services for the first time in years. Steve wondered if that was the reason he had taken up boxing and judo, so he could become good enough at both to represent the army and have something to josh with John about.

That was pointless when they were sent to Afghanistan. The sheer restriction on their life there in a compound, with continuous patrols, the heat, the sand and the bloody flies. Would he ever come to terms with that last fatal patrol? Would he ever be able forget the screaming of his injured colleagues when they had walked into that Taliban ambush? They had been clearly visible targets as they moved along that track and came under fire. Steve remembered Sergeant Bass as ever out in front. He was the first one to be hit, falling onto the track, screaming, "Take cover," as if the rest of the squad had not already dived into the ditches on either side of the track as the Taliban had planned.

The last thing Steve could clearly remember after diving into the ditch was the sound of a shattering explosion. He had no memory of what he did next, only hearing it from his surviving colleagues when they were recovering from their wounds in hospital. But all that training must have kicked in. He was told how he had climbed out of the ditch, returning fire at the approaching Taliban, and in the storm of bullets flying all around him, had stumbled his way towards Sergeant Bass and dragged him to safety into the ditch. He then apparently climbed back out of the ditch, went down on one knee, and raked the advancing line of Taliban with continuous fire until he was seen to be hit and had fallen. Others of his unit who were less wounded had recovered from the initial explosion and had joined in firing at the enemy with such fire power that the Taliban had given up the attack and retreated. The ambush had not apparently gone entirely to their plan: two of the four devices planted in the ditch had failed to detonate, otherwise it was likely death and casualties would have been much higher.

Steve remembered how he woke up to be told he was in hospital, back in England, having been in an induced coma for the last six days to help recover from his injuries. That awful, frightening feeling when he realised that he could not move his head as it was held in a brace, his right leg in plaster from the groin down to his toes held up in front of him by some sort of contraption. Steve felt the ridge of the scar that ran along the side of his head, fortunately now covered by his thick black hair. Yes, for once in his life luck had been with him; the Taliban bullet that had pierced his helmet had scored along the side of his head fracturing his skull, but had not caused any brain damage. Unfortunately the bullets they had removed from his leg had left him with a slight limp, which meant his discharge from the Army as he was too unfit to resume his career. Thoughts returned to his friend and best pal John who had not been so lucky, losing both his legs from the knee down in the original explosion, now up north somewhere, a life now without football, but helping in an institution for other injured service personnel.

CHAPTER 3

The train came to stop at Kelton Town station, the last stop before Sweetwater, only another ten minutes or so away. Steve straightened up in his seat as the train moved on. He had not told anyone of his homecoming, having been released from the court but taken into the nearby police station to answer questions over an investigation into the last prison he had been detained in. He glanced out of the window as the train approach Sweetwater. He could see Collin Cars Showroom where Julie worked and smiled to himself thinking of those early teenage romps they had together and the welcome home from the Army she gave him. Then the despair he had felt when he learnt, in prison, of her marriage. Had he really been so happy to hear that the marriage had failed, kidding himself she would be waiting for him, when, if, he ever got released. Enough memories. He stood up, hoisted his holdall over his shoulder and was waiting at the door when the train rolled into the station at Sweetwater. Thankfully there was no one there to

17

meet him. Glad he had not forwarded any details of his journey home, he left the station and walked across the forecourt out onto the road and footpath leading home. The sun had at last broken through and already he felt warmth in the air.

The loud sound of a car horn startled him and a very smart BMW motor car pulled to a stop beside him. "Need a lift, stranger?" said a voice with a laugh. He turned and looked down at the car. Julie! What a sight – long blond straight hair resting on her shoulders framing that face he would never forget, those incredible blue eyes that sparkled and glowed when she laughed. God, she was incredibly beautiful.

"What! How on earth did you know I was coming home today?" he managed to splutter out.

"Your mum got a phone message from the police station where you have been for the past few days. Someone there told her you have been helping them with some enquiry, which they would not expand on, but just said you were on your way home. She phoned me. We have been a lot closer since you have been away. I told her not to worry, I would meet both trains due from Kelton that would be arriving this afternoon. You had to be on one of them, so I took the afternoon off and here you are. Are you not pleased to see me?" she said, with a teasing expression on her face.

He realised he was standing there with an open mouth, just staring at her.

"Come on! Get in before you get lockjaw."

All he could think of was how gorgeous she looked, far from the skinny, wisp of a girl he knew, which seem to be a lifetime ago. He got into the passenger seat, tossing his holdall over his shoulder onto the back seat, and as he did so he leaned towards her and gave her a quick kiss on her cheek .

She turned and smiled, "Straight home, or coffee, tea, or something stronger at my place?"

"Your place sounds fine," he replied, not wanting to take his eyes off her for one second.

"OK, my place it is. I have a flat above the shops in the high street now, a wedding present from my mum and dad. Luckily it turned out the flat needed intensive renovation so we lived in my old flat above the showroom while the work was done. There was one problem after another concerning the new flat, which took so long to sort out my marriage ended before we had the chance to move in.

"Living above the showroom suited Malcolm, my ex. He could communicate with Carl more easily as he had become Carl's right hand man. In fact, he spent more time with Carl than he did with me. They were involved in some business together which I never found out what, very hush hush.

"And another thing, Malcolm was never interested in sex. He was always too tired or had an early morning start, or spent days away with Carl dealing with private matters concerning their business."

"It sounds as if it worked all right for Carl," said Steve. "You don't think there was more to their relationship than work?"

Julie looked at Steve, "Gosh, no! I never gave it much thought, although now you mention it I often wondered why Carl never had any girlfriends."

She drove round the back of the parade of shops and parked in what he supposed was her designated spot. They left her car and climbed the iron stairs that led to a balcony and her flat. He was not surprised to see all the walls in the flat coloured in a soft shade of pink and the carpets throughout in a darker shade. Pink had always been her favourite colour. He followed her around as she showed off the flat, unable to take his eyes off her, and what she was wearing: a white, short sleeve v-neck top and a very short pleated pink skirt. He was embarrassed to realise he was getting an erection, so he took his holdall from his shoulder and carried it in front of him. They eventually ended up in a beautiful and well equipped kitchen. Pale grey granite worktops on both sides. On the left, under the worktop, were base units with gloss white doors and gold coloured round handles. Above the work top were matching wall units. On the right, under the worktop stood a fridge, freezer and washing machine. Above the counter a large widow let in ample light. At the far end of the kitchen opposite the kitchen door was a sink unit with draining boards on both sides. A beautiful large landscape painting hung on the wall above.

In the centre of the kitchen was a small oblong table with two chairs on either side. He placed his holdall on the table.

"Tea, coffee or a beer?" she asked.

"Coffee's fine, black," he replied.

He watched her fill a kettle and reach up to one of the wall units with one hand while steadying herself with the other on the worktop. As she did so, her skirt rose up displaying more of her well-shaped and tanned thighs. He moved up behind her and placed both hands on her shoulders. He felt her bottom push back and wiggle against his already firm erection. He moved his hands from her shoulders and pushed them under her armpits and placed them on her breasts. Both her hands were now on the work top. He fondled her breasts gently, feeling her nipples harden.

"Are you sure you want do this?" he said in a very shaky voice.

"Oh yes," he heard her say and her wiggles increased against him.

He removed his hands from her breasts, eased back from her, making enough room to lift her skirt over her hips, revealing white cotton briefs. He pushed them down and slid his right hand between her legs. She was so moist his fingers easily slipped inside. To encourage him further she opened her legs wider. He removed his hand, undid his belt and dropped his jeans and pants. He took hold of his throbbing engorged penis and slid it gently into her. Their panting was almost in unison, his thrusts became quicker, each thrust seeming to lift her up onto her toes, and her hips over the top of the worktop. He shuddered violently as he climaxed. His legs were threatening to give way, his limp penis slipped from her as he stepped back and pulled up his pants and jeans, and with trembling knees he reached behind him, grabbing a chair from the table, turning it around and slumping down on it.

A great feeling of shame and despair filled him as he watched her wipe herself and re-dress. What had he done? He leaned forward placing his elbows on his knees and both hands over his face.

"I'm sorry, so sorry," he said between his fingers. He was aware of her kneeling down in front him. He felt her hands on top of his, and gently moving them apart, brushing the tears from the corner of his eyes with her thumbs.

"Why are you sorry? It's not as if this was the first time we've had sex."

"No, but I can't believe we've only just met after years apart and I lost control of myself."

She laughed. "It was the same for me! We must have something in common. Now, about that coffee..."

He stood up doing up his jeans and belt. "Are you going to be OK?"

Understanding what he meant she replied, "Yes, don't worry. I've been on the pill ever since I went into that disastrous marriage."

They sat at the table next to each other sipping their coffee. Julie had one hand on the table, and Steve placed his on top of hers and gave a gentle squeeze.

"When I came home from the army I had no thought of what my future held. Working with my dad at the timber yard was definitely not in my mind, but the light job they offered, working mainly in the office taking orders, checking invoices, and delivering instruction to the men working in the yard, was just what I needed to help my leg recover from my injuries and to get fit again. This time I really have to think hard about my future. I might see if I can get my old job back at Tunes. I have a lot more mechanical knowledge from my time in the army and I can't see your brother objecting to me working there now as we are both adults and can have a relationship with any one we like."

They kissed again and then she asked, "I'm not clear about one thing. How did that woman from France suddenly appear at your appeal?"

"Why? Not jealous already are you? No seriously, the police never believed my alibi that I left after rowing with Jackie, you know, the girl I was convicted of murdering. She was never my girlfriend. She was the daughter of The Raven owners, and I had met her several times when I had a drink there. You remember it was at that time you were with your cousins on the round-the-world trip. Jackie and I dated a couple of times, nothing serious, but she wanted more. That's what we were arguing about when the witness saw us. I made it clear to her I was not interested in anything other than being friends and walked off. I took my usual way home taking the short cut across the field, and I met that woman from France as she was also out walking. She had been staying with her husband at The Raven for one night. Apparently she came to England to a wine festival and to visit an old pen friend who seriously ill with breast cancer living in that care home, the one about a mile past your dad's car showroom. It was there that a nurse mentioned to her she could take a pleasant walk across the fields, over the river and return to The Raven along the road. What the nurse did not mention to her was that to cross the river was by means of a single plank. I was standing on the plank when I saw her approach and she seemed nervous when she realised the only way to cross the river was by that plank. I remember offering my hand, which after hesitating she accepted, and I led her across. We hardly spoke. She thanked me and we walked together across the field towards the road. I left her when I reached the gate to my garden, said good night, and that's the last I saw of her until my appeal hearing. She told the judges that she and her husband had gone back to France early the following morning, completely unaware of the terrible murder."

"OK, I understand that part. But how come the police didn't trace her at the time?"

"I'm convinced they never bothered to look that hard. They had me, witnesses to us rowing in the car park and then my blood-stained jacket found close to her body. The witnesses told the police I was wearing that jacket, they obviously did not see me give it to Jackie. They knew it was my jacket, cause my bloody credit card and driving licence were in a breast pocket. I keep thinking, if the French woman's friend had not died, she would never had reason to return to England and I would still be serving a life sentence. Anyway, she came to her friend's funeral and stayed again at The Raven, now with new owners. After my conviction, Jackie's parents sold up and moved away. You can understand why. Let's have another coffee and I'll tell you the rest of the story."

Julie hurriedly made the coffee while Steve used her toilet. When he returned Julie informed him she had phoned his mum, telling her she had collected him from the station and they were having coffee, discussing old times, not to worry as he would be home shortly. He thanked her.

"Where shall I start?" asked Steve. "Have you not heard this before?"

"No, only hearsay. I was in the back of the court, but seeing you was too much for me so I left before she gave her evidence to the appeal judges."

"Her name is Louise Hallet," Steve began. "She and her husband own a small winery in France, hence the visit to England and the wine festival in the first place, when she also took the opportunity to visit a very sick pen pal. When she later heard that her friend had died she felt compelled to return to Sweetwater and attend her friend's funeral. That's when my luck changed. She stayed at The Raven again, and during a conversation with the new owners, learnt how they came to buy The Raven. This piqued her interest and subsequently she contacted the police. Louise was able to be so clear about what she witnessed that night for a number of reasons. After dinner at The Raven her husband had retired to bed stating he needed his sleep before the early morning start and long drive home the next day. Louise told him she was going for a walk for some fresh air before bed. She left the building and as she crossed the car park she was aware of two people, male and female, having an argument at one end of the car park. She saw the man take of his jacket and offer it to the woman who put it on. The man was left wearing a plain white long sleeve T shirt. That made her realise there was a chill in the air and she returned to her room to get a cardigan. Back in her room she used the toilet, had a conversation with her husband and then exited the building again. This time she was nearly run over by a car leaving the car park. She described the car as being a dark coloured saloon, possibly a Mercedes, with the most striking bright shining silver or chrome spoked wheels, similar to cycle wheels. As she stepped back from its path, she saw the woman who had previously been arguing with the other man sitting in the passenger seat, easily recognisable by the jacket she had seen the man give her. She could not see who was driving this car, nor did she note the car number plate. The car turned right from the car park and she continued her walk in the opposite direction with the intention of following the route given to her early that day by the nurse at the care home. Walking along the footpath beside the road, she was aware of the light falling and at the gate leading into the field was the second reason she had such a good memory of the evening. Opening the gate she saw what she could only described as an apparition, a figure, about thirty or so meters from her, hovering above the river. Curiosity got the better of her and she walked slowly along the path towards the figure until she realised the figure was the man she recognised as me, standing on a plank across the river. Fortunately she also identified me as the man arguing with the woman in the car park. As I had told the police in my statement. We spoke, and she was nervous about stepping onto the plank to cross the river. She actually laughed as I walked backwards leading her across. I think she made a comment about my T shirt and how it had stood out when she entered the field giving her the false impression I was hovering above the river. We walked together up to my home and parted. I watched her join the road, and that was the last I saw of her until my appeal.

"The problem for me was she never told me who she was or what she was doing here, so I was unable to help the police find her. Thankfully the judges believed her account of that night which fully supported my alibi.

"That's enough of me talking. I'd better be off home or Mum will be worried. I'll walk if you don't mind. I'm dying to see the bridge which has replaced the old plank across the river. I'm going to need some time to sort myself out, visit the bank, arrange for a new credit card and buy a mobile phone. Give me a couple of days and I'll contact you again."

Julie stood up from the table pointing her finger, "You'd better, or I'll tell my brother how you've had your wicked way with me." Laughing, she put her arms round him and they kissed passionately.

They broke apart, Steve hoisted his holdall onto his shoulder and said, "From now on I don't care who you tell about us. I'm never letting anything, or anyone spoil our relationship." He waved to her as he left the flat.

Julie watched him leave, thinking about what had happened between them and of the extraordinary story he had just related to her. She smiled to herself when she remembered how she had deliberately worn a short skirt to meet him, the way she had flaunted herself when showing him around the flat and stretching up higher than she needed at the cupboard, knowing he was behind her and would be looking at her legs. At that moment she could have stopped it going any further but then, as she felt him behind her, she realised she wanted him to make love to her. She had needed to know that her marriage had not changed the way he felt about her. Yes, she had taken a chance. She knew that after being locked up for four years, any man would be glad of a willing woman, but his attitude after the sex dispelled any doubts about his feelings for her.

CHAPTER 4

Leaving the flat, walking round the rear of the buildings and across the road, Steve thought of how shattered he had been when his mother told him of Julie's marriage. He had to come to terms with that news. Did he really expect her to remain single for the rest of her life? News of her divorce reached him at the same time his solicitor informed him of his appeal date. That's when he first began to have hope that things may be turning in his favour. What had happened in her flat had been completely unexpected, but he now knew without any doubt that she loved him.

Reaching the gate leading to the footpath across the field, he could see the bridge in the distance. Opening the gate, a shaft of sunshine seem to strike the bridge, lighting it up as if it was on display. He strolled along the footpath, across the field and up to the bridge. He stood still at first, not wanting to step onto it, and looking down at the floor he was surprised to see the old plank was still there as part of the new bridge.

Two other planks had been attached on either side and from these wooden rounded railings stretched up to oval shape hand rails. Stepping onto the bridge he was struck by a dazzling light that glistened from a point in the centre of a hand rail. Moving forward he saw the light was reflecting off a brass plaque which bore the inscription, 'In Loving Memory Of Martin Day'. Tears flooded from his eyes at the memory of his brother's tragic death at this spot so many years ago. He kissed two fingers and gently touched his brother's name.

Turning he left the bridge and walked up to the gate into his garden. As he opened the gate the back door of the house opened and his mother appeared. She walked down the garden towards him arms outstretched. They embraced, both crying uncontrollably, then his father was there hugging them both, saying, "Welcome home, son."

When they were able to separate they made their way into the cottage where his mum took charge. "I've prepared your favourite meal to welcome you home. It will be ready in about an hour, so there's time for you to have a shower. Your room has been ready since your appeal. I don't understand why the police have kept you for so long."

"Don't worry, Mum. It's a long story, but now it's all cleared up. I'm home! This time to stay."

CHAPTER 5

Dinner that night was bangers, mash, and onion gravy. He shared a few bottles of beer with his father and retired early saying he was tired after the long journey home, and thinking that was not all that had tired him. After breakfast the next morning, his dad already left for work, he told his mum he was going to spend the day sorting out the bank. He needed to get new credit cards, a mobile phone and some new clothes.

"Yes, I expected that, you've filled out a lot. What were they feeding you on in prison?"

He shrugged his shoulders. "The food was OK, but I spent a lot of time in the gym, something to do to pass the time." Grabbing his jacket, he made for the door, then as an afterthought he called out, "Don't worry about lunch. I'll get something out."

His mum gave him a hug and kiss, saying, "Take care."

He left via the back garden, through the gate and across the field, taking the short cut to the village.

Over the bridge he again kissed his fingers and touched Martin's plaque, and this time he was able to hold onto his emotions.

The first stop was the bank for some money and to check his account. Entering the bank he spoke to a girl on the till asking if the manager was available. She made a phone call and a few minutes later, Mr Stubbs, the manager came out of his office, extending his hand at Steve as he walked towards him. They shook hands.

"I was not sure you would still be here, I thought you might have retired," said Steve.

"No chance of that. I'm fighting to keep this place open, what with all the closures that are going on at the moment. Come on into my office. You probably have a lot to talk about since your time in ..., I mean since you've been away."

Having made arrangements for new bank cards, which would take several days to arrive, Steve left the bank with £200 in his wallet, drawn from his savings account which due to a monthly direct debit paid from his parents' account, had grown to a healthy sum. He would speak to his parents about that later.

Next, the train to Kelton. Walking towards the station he had to pass Tunes garage and could not help looking through the open doors. James was sitting on his chair, whittling away with a mound of shavings beneath his feet. Steve saw him glance towards him, and then he did a double take as the sight registered in his confused brain. Knife and wood were thrown to the floor as he leapt from his chair and hurled himself towards Steve, jumping up, arms round his shoulders and legs round his waist.

"Steady on! You will have us both on the floor," said Steve.

Then another voice sounded out from the rear of the garage. "So the fallen hero, or is it the released convict has returned?"

Steve released James from his grasp and saw Ray Tunes move out from behind the bonnet of a car he had been working on.

"I see nothing's changed," said Steve. "Still the arrogant bastard you've always been."

The door of the garage office opened and Jake Tunes stepped out. Seeing Steve, he laughingly said, "Well, well, fancy you turning up here. Not looking to get your old job back?"

"No, not really. Just passing by and seeing if you are still in business."

"Here, just a moment. If you're interested, I might have something for you. Step into my office," Jake said.

Steve thought for a few seconds. He was tempted to say no, but then he needed a job and it would not hurt to hear what was on offer. He followed Jake into the office.

"You've come at the right time," began Jake. "It so happens that Ray has been offered a job by Carl Collins moving vehicles around their showrooms, something he is desperate to do, driving smart new top of the range BMWs all day instead of working here and getting his hands all dirty and greasy. Would you be interested in taking his place?"

Steve considered the offer. Ray was standing at the office door. "You probably won't get a better offer round here. People have long memories and some will always doubt your innocence."

Yes, that's just the sort of comment from a prat like Ray, Steve thought, and he was on the point of telling them to stuff the job, when James pushed his way past Ray into the office shouting, "Please, please, please."

Mind made up, accepting the terms offered to him and agreeing to start work come Monday, Steve left the office. As he did so, he was angered to see

Ray deliberately kick the wood shavings from under James chair across the garage floor, saying, "I'm off for an early lunch. Make sure you sweep that lot up before I return, idiot."

Steve stepped forward and then controlled his anger, bent down, took the brush from James and began sweeping the shavings into a pile. As he did so, he said in a quiet voice, "Don't worry, mate. Things will change around here come Monday." James' face lit up and he took back the brush from Steve and dropped the shavings into a nearby bin.

Steve left the garage and caught the train to Kelton. He shopped for clothing and a mobile phone. Having secured the latter on a pay as you go contract, only needing a basic model to send and receive calls, he noticed the phone had a camera, which little did he know was to become very handy later. He had lunch at a small restaurant adjacent to the station and a pint at a nearby pub, then caught the train back to Sweetwater with a bag full of new clothing and little left of the two hundred pounds he had started with.

Once home, the first thing he did was to get Julie's number from his mum and give her a call. She answered almost immediately and he related to her his morning achievements, explaining about the job offer but not the reason why he accepted. The conversation ended with a date for dinner that evening at The Raven.

CHAPTER 6

He turned up a little early for his date so he ordered a pint of a local ale, and chose a seat facing the door so he could see Julie when she arrived. He was on his second pint when the door of the bar opened and Julie entered. She spied Steve, waved and walked towards him. Steve stood up. She looked stunning, her golden blond hair hung down over her shoulders partly covering a low-slung blue blouse which dropped loose over a pair of three-quarter length pink jeans. They kissed, she sat down and he went to the bar and ordered her a small white wine. He returned with her drink and sat next to her. He could not take his eyes off her. She had developed into a very beautiful woman, far from the giggling teenager he had seduced many times on the river bank and other places years ago.

"I really need to apologise for yesterday. I should never had taken advantage of you like that. I still can't believe I did what I did," he said.

She reached forward, placing her fingers on his lips. "Quiet. It happened. I think it was something we both needed, and I for one am not sorry at all."

The following days passed quickly. He sorted out his old clothes, giving them to his mum for a local jumble sale, and spent as much time as possible with Julie. Monday came round and he started at the garage. He saw little of Ray other than him bringing in cars from Collins for service, and on several occasions seeing him in the office with what appeared to be heated discussions with Jake. He and James became very close. On the days he was not at the Community Centre, James would always be willing to do anything for Steve. Whenever Ray was at the garage, Steve made sure he was close to James to stop him from being picked on by his brother. At this time he did not know that this friendship would, in the not too distant future, save his life.

Everything in Steve's life seem to be running smoothly. He saw a lot of Julie, often spending the entire nights at her flat. His mother showed her disapproval of this, but came to accept it after he heard his father say to her, "He's a grown man. Remember what it was like when we were young and courting."

CHAPTER 7

Then came another change. One Sunday morning after a late breakfast with his parents, the front door bell sounded. Steve got up from the table to see who was calling. He opened the door. Standing in front of him was a very attractive woman, about five eight, with dark brown curly hair nestling around her ears and neck, and clear hazel eyes. She had a round face, a pointed small nose, thin lips and she wore an open neck white blouse showing off a hint of cleavage, a grey jacket and, matching it, a fairly short tight straight skirt hugging her hips and thighs.

"Seen enough?" Steve realised he was staring. Yes he had seen enough. This was the one person he would be happy to never see in his life again. Detective Inspector Janet Swift, the police officer who headed the CID unit that had been responsible for the case against him, which resulted in his conviction for the murder of the girl Jackie.

"Look," she said, "I know what you think of me and I am sorry I am disturbing you on a Sunday, but

I must talk to you. We, the police, need your help, and if you agree, it may lead us to discover who killed Jackie."

Yes, thought Steve, talk about dangling a carrot. Intrigued as to what she had to say he invited her in. He showed her into the dining room and went to inform his parents, telling them that the police were here to clear up a few outstanding matters. He returned to the DI and they sat facing each across the dining room table.

She began. "What I am about to tell you is most secret and must remain between these four walls. Do you understand that and give me your word it will remain so?"

"Yes," he replied. "So now you will take my word?"

Noticing the sting in his reply, DI Swift said, "Yes I will. I cannot make up for what happened to you but if everything falls into place you will be fully cleared of that horrendous crime and help once and for all to prove to those disbelievers that you had nothing to do with that murder.

"First let me explain. I know all about your involvement in the trouble at the last prison you were in. Those prison officers whom you identified, bullying inmates and running drug and mobile phone rackets for cash or favours, have now been suspended and will face criminal charges."

"Hang on there," interrupted Steve. "I was given assurance that my name would be kept out of the investigation, yet here you are knowing all about it. How can I believe anything you lot say?"

"You don't have to worry. Your name came up at a Police Superintendent Conference. My Super heard of the help you gave to the authorities and it's that kind of help I am going to ask for in our investigation on another matter. May I continue?"

"I think I'm going to need some coffee. I'm not sure where this is going. Would you like a drink?" asked Steve.

"Coffee would be fine, milk no sugar."

Steve left the room and returned a few minutes later. "Right, that's organised."

"I've been thinking while you were out of the room," said the DI. "I've let things get ahead a bit. I need to fill you in on several very important matters that are not public knowledge and must remain that way for the time being."

The door opened and Steve's mum entered with a tray on which were mugs of steaming coffee. "Anything else I can get you?" she asked.

"No, Mum. This is going to take longer than expected but there is nothing for you to worry about. We're just clearing up police bureaucracy."

"Alright, I'll leave you to it. Shout if you need anything," she said, and left the room.

"This is the bit I should have told you earlier," explained the DI. "Three months ago, the partly decomposed body of a young woman was found by a dog walker in the river Swee where it runs under a railway bridge outside Kelton. First thoughts were that she must have been hit by a train. The PM showed otherwise. She had been strangled and stabbed many times in the chest. A few days ago we got the full forensic report. The knife marks on her ribs were identical to those found on Jackie, meaning it was highly probable it was the same knife. Obviously if we find the knife then forensics will be able to make a perfect match."

Steve stared at her, trying to absorb this information. Finding his voice he said, with a smile on his face, "Well, you'll not be able to pin that one on me, as I was a guest at Her Majesty's prison."

She smiled back. "Let me continue. The girl has been identified as Donna Geer who came to live in Kelton after a messy divorce up in Scotland. We do know she worked at Collin Cars but disappeared several weeks before her body was found. It was thought she had returned to Scotland so no one reported her missing. I am telling you all this because after the statement from Louise the woman from France, we have been trying to identify the car she saw leaving the car park with Jackie. We now know a Mercedes of a similar description was reported stolen from Collin Cars two days after Jackie's body was found. We have interviewed several witness who have stated that they had seen Carl Collins driving that car days prior to it being reported stolen. Like the knife, we need to find the car to help with our enquiries."

The DI stopped, and then said, "I am not one who believes in coincidences, but it seems possible that Collin Cars has in some way been involved in the murder of both Jackie and Donna. Now I come to the point as to why I am telling you all this and why we are seeking your assistance. Over the past year the National Crime Unit have been investigating the theft of high quality vehicles from around the country. This is the bit that concerns you. They have identified Collin Cars and Tunes garage as being involved in the handling of some of these stolen vehicles."

"Jesus Christ," exclaimed Steve. "Are you saying I am involved in vehicle theft?"

"No, not at all. We know you are working at Tunes and we hope, hearing all that I have explained, you will consent to help us by keeping your eyes open and reporting to us, me, anything that is suspicious, like expensive vehicles appearing at the garage that don't fit the day to day work that you are normally involved with."

A horrid thought crossed Steve's mind. Is Julie somehow involved in this, and if not, what would she think of him working with the police as a snitch. "You are asking me to do this purely because of the way I assisted in the prison business, which I only did because of the way I saw certain prisoners being treated. This is entirely different. What you are asking me to do is to become an informer. I'm not sure about this. I guess that is why you have shared with me the information about the knife, car, and the connection with Collin Cars hoping I will agree." Steve sat back in his chair and waited for the DI's response.

"Let me be clear," she began, "It's not my call to involve you in this, but time is of the essence. A lot of work has been done by police throughout the country to stop these thefts and to bring the culprits to justice.

If one word gets out that we are on to them, they will shut down and all the hard work would have been for nothing. My Superintendent, hearing of your involvement with the prison business, has instructed me to approach you and seek your help, you being in the right place at the right time. Do you understand that?"

"Of course I do. I'm not an idiot. Just tell me what you want from me," Steve snapped back.

"You don't have to get involved other than to take photos of any vehicle which you are suspicious of, making sure you include the registration number, and forwarding details to me on my private mobile. What do you say?"

Christ, Steve thought. If he agreed and Julie found out he had been working with the police in providing evidence against her brother and the family business, how would she ever forgive him?

"I need time to think about it," uttered Steve. "What I can tell you is that on several occasions when I have arrived for work I have noticed a very expensive looking vehicle in the garage which was quickly removed by Ray Tunes, who explained he was in the process of moving it from one of Collin Cars premises to another as it was normal business practice to move stock around. If I do agree to do this, will you keep my name out of any further police action?"

"All we need is to catch them with a stolen vehicle in their possession. You can leave the rest to us. I will be your only contact, and no one else will know of your involvement."

"OK, I'll do what I can," replied Steve. They both rose from the table and as Steve saw her to the door, she passed him her private personal contact card and left. He returned to his parents. "That's all sorted, a few details that needed to be cleared up, and with luck that will be the last I see of her."

CHAPTER 8

Later that morning Steve told his mother he was off to meet Julie and would be taking her for lunch at The Raven. He left, taking his usual route across the fields over the bridge into the village. Walking towards The Raven, he noticed one of the Tunes' garage shutters was open, which was unusual for a Sunday. He made his way to the garage and looked inside. He was surprised to see a brilliant red coloured Honda CRV motor vehicle which had not been there when he finished work the day before. The vehicle was obviously brand new as he could see there was still clear plastic sheeting covering the seats. He glanced at the registration plate which he realised was four years old. This was odd, as the vehicle and plate did not match. He took out his mobile and took photos, sending them straight to DI Swift's mobile. Surely it was not going to be as easy as this, he thought. He had only seen the DI a few hours ago. Curiously he looked through the driver's side window and saw there were only two hundred miles registered as mileage.

"Hi! What are you doing here?" called out Ray Tune emerging from the office.

"Just being inquisitive," Steve replied. "I saw the shutter was open so checked to see if everything was OK."

"Yes it's fine. Dropped the Honda off yesterday evening for someone to collect it today, a surprise birthday present for some lucky bastard. I've been here for the last hour waiting for it to be collected, something to do with Carl Collins, nothing for you to worry about."

"Fair enough. I'll leave you to it," called out Steve, who turned and walked off wondering why there was an old number plate on a brand new vehicle. Still, he had done his bit and would let DI Swift do the rest.

Steve made his way to The Raven and entered the saloon bar. He ordered a pint, and turning around saw Julie sitting at a table with a man. The man's back was towards him, and they seem to be in an earnest conversation. Julie saw him and rose from the table. The man rose too and leaned forward, planting a kiss on Julie's cheek. He then turned and walked past Steve towards the door. Steve noted he was about six feet tall, slim, dark brown hair, well groomed. He had a long face, small pointed nose and a thin beard down the side of his face and around his chin. He was smartly dressed in a light grey suit, white shirt and blue tie.

"Before you ask," spoke Julie, who was walking towards him, "that's Malcolm, my ex. We bumped into each other outside. He's on his way to Tunes to collect a vehicle and deliver to the new owner at a surprise 60th birthday party."

Steve ordered some drinks and they went and sat at a table. "Do you see much of him?" inquired Steve.

"He works at the showrooms, moving around, filling in when staff are on holiday, sick or shorthanded. Why? Does it bother you? Let me explain. It was a big mistake by both of us getting married. Me, because I was in shock, gutted, or whatever you want to call it, when you were sentenced to life imprisonment. He, because he was never in love with me but had become very friendly with my brother in a big way and saw a way of becoming part of Collin Cars, his future secure. At that time I was too easily manipulated and think my brother saw it as a way of getting me out of the way. Anyway it happened, we married and it did not take long for both of us to realise what a huge mistake we had made, hence how quickly we divorced."

Steve sat there watching her face as she spoke. "I've always disliked your brother, even more so now after what you've just told me."

"Let me tell you something," Julie replied. "It's not common knowledge, but he's not my real brother. My parents adopted him when he was quite small as they had not been able to conceive a child of their own. Like a lot of parents in that situation, four years after the adoption, a miracle occurred and my mother got pregnant with me. Carl has no love for me, he takes every opportunity to put me down. Things are different now with you behind me," she broke off, giggling. "I mean, now we are together, he leaves me alone. I run the business with my dad and he seems to do whatever he wants, especially as he and Malcolm are now back working together again."

Steve's phone vibrated against his leg, "I think that's enough of family talk, let's get a table in the restaurant. I'm starving."

They entered the restaurant and Steve made his excuses to go to the toilet. Once there he checked his phone, and saw a message from DI Swift informing him that the Honda vehicle checked out. His wife knew about the present and wanted to keep her old number plate. Steve returned to the restaurant thinking over what Julie had told him about Carl. No love lost there. He realised that if he was responsible in some way for providing evidence against Carl, he did not have to worry about Julie's feelings as long as she was not involved.

Having enjoyed their meal they returned to her flat, had coffee and then retired to her bedroom. They both undressed and lay together on the bed. They began kissing and fondling each other, he caressing her breasts, first with his fingers and then being more aroused with his tongue. She responded, rubbing her hands over his stomach and onto his erection. Lifting herself above him she straddled his legs and guided his penis inside her. She moved slowly at first up and down whilst looking directly into his eyes. Her movements quickened, he arched his back pushing himself deep inside her, but as his pace increased she stopped and rolled off him dragging him on top of her. Taking her in this position, he placed his hands on either side of her shoulders and kissed her passionately as they both climaxed together.

With a shuddering breath, he moved off her onto his back. His breathing returning to normal he turned to face her and said, "You know I really do love you."

She smiled, "I love you too." They kissed, and holding each other fell into a deep sleep.

When Steve woke up, he saw the bed was empty and then the smell of fresh coffee reached him. He rose from the bed. "I'm going for a shower," he called out. Having showered and dressed, he went into the kitchen and sat with Julie drinking the coffee. They did not speak as they were quite content just being together.

He glanced at his watch. It was 7.30pm, they had slept all afternoon. "I'd better be going, got an early start tomorrow and I need my strength," he said, laughing at the same time. He kissed her saying, "I'll walk home. The fresh air will do me good."

Over the next few weeks things at the garage seem normal. Steve and Julie had provided James with some early reading books which he was enjoying. These books had pictures and little words to help him learn the alphabet. When at the garage James loved to try reading out loud to Steve, calling for help when he could not understand a word. Steve loved to help and encourage him, and would often take his break sitting beside him.

His relationship with Julie was now very intense and he believed they might have a permanent future together. He thought of their fling as teenagers, her visiting him and writing to him in prison, and of course his parents adored her. Her father did not seem to be against their relationship but her brother was always going to be a problem.

The following weeks passed without anything out of the ordinary happening. Several times when he started work in the morning there would be fairly new vehicles of different makes parked inside the garage that had not been there when he had finished the night before. These, he was informed by Jake, had only been left overnight by Ray, who was using them as transport shuffling them from one Collins showroom to another. He took pictures of these vehicles whenever possible and passed the information to DI Swift. He had no feedback from her so assumed they were all in order. Then, when arriving for work one morning he was met by Jake who came out of the office saying, "There's a Range Rover that's broken down along Sandhurst Lane. Take the breakdown truck and bring it back here." He handed the keys to Steve.

"Right. Can James come with me? It would do him good to see how we work," Steve replied.

"Fine, but make sure he stays in the cab," replied Jake.

James who was sitting on his seat, jumped up, excitement written all over his face. He had never been taken on any previous recovery jobs. Steve helped James into the recovery vehicle cab and they set off. Driving along Sandhurst Lane they soon found the Range Rover. The vehicle was the latest model with the current year's registration. The front nearside was leaning downwards, the wheel being in a deep pothole. Telling James to stay in the vehicle, he got out and went to speak to a young man who was leaning on the bonnet of the Rover. The man straightened up and said, "Guess I'm in the shit. I swerved to miss a fox and hit two bloody great potholes, both nearside tyres burst, and there's only one spare. I changed the rear wheel and called your garage with the number Carl Collins gave me in case I got in trouble. He's not going to be very happy with me. I was just delivering this vehicle for a friend who became ill at the last moment." The man then introduced himself as Tony.

"No problem," replied Steve, taking out his mobile. "Just a few snaps, company policy, in case we get accused of any damage during the recovery." He made sure the photos covered the number plate, as he was now suspicious of how a spanking new vehicle was being delivered to Collins by someone doing a favour for a so-called friend. Having hitched the Range Rover to the recovery vehicle, they made their way back to the garage. Tony sat in the cab between Steve and James, and during the journey Tony had a friendly conversation with James pointing out several birds and flowers as they passed along the hedges on the sides of the lane. If he was aware that James was a bit slow he made no comment, and when they arrived at the garage he and James were talking and laughing like old friends.

Before Steve could alight from the cab, Jake came out with a clipboard. Giving it to Steve, he told him to take the Rover straight up to Collins, as Carl said he would deal with the burst tyre. "Make sure you get a signature on the work sheet, as this is the first time Carl has said he would deal with the problem himself, and knowing him he will try to avoid paying for the recovery."

This gets more interesting thought Steve as he drove to Collin Cars Showroom. He pulled up outside the main entrance and was met by Carl who shouted at Steve, "Not here! Round the back." Steve did as he was told and was surprised to find there were two single garages at the rear of the building. The doors on one garage were open but the other was closed. Alongside the garages was a large shipping container with the doors also closed.

"Back the Rover into that garage," shouted Carl. With Tony helping, Steve did so. He then drove back round to the front, and, telling James to stay in the cab, went into the building to get the work sheet signed. There was no sign of Carl, but Julie was at the desk, and seeing Steve, rose up and went to him.

"This is a nice surprise. What are you doing here?"

"I've delivered a vehicle for your brother and need a signature on this work sheet," replied Steve, giving her a hug and kiss.

"Here, give it to me," Julie signed the sheet, and as she did so there was a loud scream from outside.

They both rushed out of the building to see James lying beside the front wheel of the recovery vehicle with blood streaming down his face. Standing over him, laughing, were Ray Tunes and Carl.

"What the hell happened here?" yelled Steve.

"Idiot fell out of the cab," smirked Ray.

"No, he did not! I saw it all. You just pulled him out," called out Tony, who was walking towards them.

"You shut your fucking mouth, I'll deal with you later," shrieked Carl.

Julie was helping James to his feet, holding a handkerchief to his face. "He has a bad gash on his forehead that will require stitching. I'll take him to the hospital at Kelton." With her arm around James, she led him towards her car parked nearby.

"Which of you bastards pulled him out of the cab?" asked Steve.

"They both did," said Tony. "They opened the cab door and grabbed him."

"Mind your own fucking business. Keep out of this, if you know what's good for you," raged Carl.

"I've heard enough," Steve said, turning towards Ray. "You've always hated your brother, teasing him and calling names. Well, this time you've gone too far." He went to grab him but was grabbed from behind by Carl and only just managed to avoid being punched in the face by him. Carl's face was red with rage and he again swung his fist at Steve. This was what Steve had waited for, he parried the blow and then hit Carl in the midriff, and as he folded over winded, Steve brought his fist up, landing it right on Carl's chin who fell to the ground.

"Look out," shouted Tony. Steve spun round. Ray was advancing towards him swinging a large chain which he had taken off the back of the recovery truck. Ray swung the chain at Steve who ducked, and it swished over his head, crashing against the side of the recovery vehicle. Steve was able to grab the end of the chain and pulled Ray forward, as he did so he hit Ray straight in the face with his fist. Ray staggered backwards dropped the chain and fell onto his back blood streaming down his face from his nose.

"Get up, you cowardly bastard. This is not finished yet."

Steve then heard Julie yelling out as she drove past on her way to the hospital. "Go! Just go. I'll contact you later."

Tony came up to him. "No point me staying round here. I don't think I'm going to get paid. Can you give me a lift to the nearest railway station?"

CHAPTER 9

Steve could see that both Ray and Carl were not in any fit state to continue the fight so told Tony to get into the recovery vehicle. He took Tony to the station. Before they parted Tony gave him his mobile number in case he needed a witness to what had occurred at Collins. Steve then sent the details of the Range Rover to DI Swift before making his way back to the garage, dreading what he was going to tell Jake. Arriving at the garage he parked the recovery vehicle at the back and with the keys and clipboard went to the office to speak to Jake. He related to him the details of James' 'accident' but declined to mention exactly how the injury to him had occurred, or the fight he had with Ray and Carl.

Jake did not seem to be concerned about James, accepting that he was being treated at the hospital and was in Julie's care. "The exhaust system for the Toyota has arrived. Can you get on with that"? called Jake.

Steve drove the Toyota onto the hydraulic lift, raised the vehicle and began working under it, removing the old exhaust. He had finished the job and was about to lower the vehicle to the ground when Ray came storming into the garage. Steve could see his nose was red and swollen. He glared at Steve and went straight into the office. Cleaning his hands and at the same time trying to keep his eye on what was happening with Ray and Jake, Steve saw that Ray was constantly raising his arms and pointing towards him. Both Ray and Jake came out and called Steve over.

"Did you do that to him?" said Jake, pointing at Ray's face.

"Yes, I certainly did, and if he had got up from the ground I would have hit him a few times more after he pulled James out of the recovery cab, assaulting him."

"No, I didn't, you bloody liar. He fell out and I tried to catch him," screamed Ray.

Steve took out his mobile and waved it at Jake. "If you want the truth of what happened, call the lad Tony who was delivering the Range Rover. He saw the whole thing."

Ray made a grab for the phone but only managed to knock it to the ground. He then made an attempt to smash the phone with his shoe, but Jake stopped him. Suddenly there was a squeal of brakes and a BMW skidded to halt at the front of the garage. Carl Collins got out of the vehicle and strode purposely towards them, with anger written all over his face.

"We're in deep trouble. The fucking police are all over the showrooms. They have seized that Rover and I only managed to avoid them by the skin on my teeth," roared Carl. "Someone must have tipped them off, and I think he's the culprit," he said, pointing at Steve. "Grab him! I'll teach him a lesson he'll never forget."

Before Steve could react, his arms were held firmly by Ray and Jake. Carl came forward and smashed his fist into Steve's stomach, knocking all three of them backwards. "Hold him still you fuckers, that's just for starters." Carl raised his fist to hit Steve again but Steve was ready for him, and as Carl reached for him, Steve lashed out with his leg, catching Carl straight between the legs. With a gasp of anguish Carl staggered back, his hands clasping his groin. Steve tried to escape from Ray and Jake but they held him fast. Carl slowly recovered and seeing James' knife beside him on a chair, he grabbed it and holding it in front of him, lunged at Steve with a scream. Ray panicked and released Steve who, as the knife came towards him, managed to turn sideways so the knife struck him on his shoulder instead of his chest. Pain engulfed him. He heard a snapping sound, then something struck him on the head and he fell to the ground unconscious.

CHAPTER 10

When Steve woke, both his hands were tied behind his back, his feet were lashed together and tape had been stuck across his mouth. He tried raising his head but that brought waves of giddiness and shooting pains to his head. His shoulder felt it was on fire and throbbed where he had been stabbed. He tried several time to roll onto his good shoulder but that just piled on the agony from his wounds. He was in almost complete darkness. What light there was came from two small cracks in the ceiling way in front of him and was not enough to make out where he was. He lay still, trying to remember what had happened to him. He remembered the knife in Carl's hand and the triumph on his face as he stabbed him, and then nothing. His hands had gone numb so he tried arching his back to relieve some of the pressure on them. The agonising pain from his shoulder meant he could only hold the position for a few minutes but he could feel tingling returning to his fingers.

How long had he been unconscious? Where was he? Surely he must have been missed. People must be looking for him. The tape across his mouth made it impossible to move his lips. He tried hard to make a cry or sound, but was unable to do so. He tried bending his knees and stamping his feet but that hardly made a sound. He carefully moved his feet first to his right until they stopped against an obstruction, and then back to his left, again until they hit something solid. He realised he was in some sort of narrow space no more than three feet wide. He drifted between periods of sleep and consciousness. Sometimes when awake he thought he could hear voices, but was unsure if he was dreaming. Thirst was always with him, his mouth was constantly dry: rolling his tongue around he could only manage a small amount of saliva. He thought of Julie and his parents. If he died here, would they ever find his body? Despair overcame him, he could do nothing to free himself and he was growing weaker and weaker. Time had no meaning, only pain, thirst and darkness during periods of awareness.

When all seemed lost, he was roused by a scraping noise, light flooded in, he raised his head and torchlight struck his face, then a voice shouted out, "There's someone down here! I can see his head moving." At that he passed into unconsciousness again. Was this a dream? He could feel someone stroking his hand. He was laying on something very soft and comfortable. He open his eyes and brightness struck him, causing him to blink rapidly. Then he was able to clearly see a white ceiling above and heard a voice calling out, "He's awake."

It was Julie's voice. One he thought he would never hear again. He realised he was in a bed, his arms were in front of him and they were attached to tubes rising to stands on either side of him. It's a hospital bed, he registered. "Water," he croaked.

His head was lifted gently and a spout or tube was placed between his lips. He sucked greedily until a voice said, "Slowly. Just a little at a time." Then Julie was leaning over him. "You're safe, darling, but you need to keep still. You've had surgery on your shoulder and there are stitches." He looked up to her face and tried to smile but even that was an effort and he closed his eyes and slept.

CHAPTER 11

The next few days were a blur, with regular visits by his parents, Julie and DI Swift. He was able to relate to DI Swift the attack on him by Carl Collins helped by Jake and Ray Tunes. He was clear that it was Carl who had stabbed him but he was unable to recount what happened to him up until he woke up in that dark place. He was then told that he had been found in the old disused inspection pit under the garage floor which had been boarded over when the Tunes had the hydraulic lift installed.

The DI also told him that the two Tune brothers were in custody but there was no trace of Carl Collins who was now wanted for attempted murder. Pain from his shoulder gradually lessened, his wrists were sore and deeply lacerated from his struggles to get free from the ties that had been used to bind them. His face was also sore from the tape, and talking was an effort. The doctor in charge of him explained that the blade of a knife had been removed from his left shoulder, he had been lucky. The blade had gone over the top of his collar bone but had not struck anything vital. When admitted he had been seriously dehydrated and that had been very concerning, but the doctor was pleased with his recovery and Steve should be able to go home within the next few days. Steve thought about the knife. He realised that if the blade had not snapped off then Carl may have used it again to stab him in a more vital place. His recovery progressed fairly quickly, and he was allowed out of bed to sit in a comfortable chair.

Julie came every day and on one visit brought James with her. With a small plaster on his forehead and with a massive grin on his face it was all Julie could do to stop him hurling himself at Steve. "Hi mate," said Steve, holding out his good arm to shake James hand. "It's so nice to see you."

"I think he deserves more than a handshake: if it wasn't for him you might never have been found," said Julie, who then went on to relate to Steve how James had been instrumental in finding him. "When I returned from the hospital with James having had his head stitched, the police were all over the place, the showroom was closed, all the staff sent home, and Carl's flat, above the showroom, was a scene of activity by policemen, some in white overalls. Your friend," she said smiling, "DI Swift was in charge, and told me they were investigating a nationwide gang of vehicle thefts and they believed Carl was involved with Jake and Ray Tunes who were both in custody, but they could find no trace of Carl who had obviously done a runner. I took James home and went to the garage to find you but the garage was shut and I assumed you had gone home. I had to sort things out with the police and it was much later that evening that your mum rang me to ask if you were with me as you had not returned from work and she had not heard from you. I told DI Swift you were missing and the shit hit the fan. Apparently Jake Tunes, trying to distance himself from you, told the police he saw you drive off with Carl shortly before the police arrived at the garage."

Steve looked at Julie and nodded towards James. "How did he become involved?"

"Of course you don't know this, but after Jake and Ray were arrested, James was put into a foster home in Kelton. After a few days he made such a fuss about his books being left in the garage, that his foster parents contacted the police to ask their help in collecting the books. They sent a car to pick him up and take him to the garage, which was still taped off as part of the police enquiries. The police let James into the garage, and as he picked up his books he became agitated because his knife was missing. He got down on his knees and looked under the car which was on the hydraulic lift in the down position. He shouted to the police that he could see the handle of his knife under the car. So to calm him down they moved the car and saw that several pieces of board on the garage floor had been moved recently. They lifted the boards and, thank God, found you!"

"I suppose that in getting me out of sight before the police arrived, Carl must have thrown the broken off handle of the knife away and it landed under the car and wasn't noticed by them when they moved the car from the lift, put me in the pit and then replaced the car to cover up what they had done. Well, James, but for your actions I might still be in that pit. Something I promise you I am never going to forget."

CHAPTER 12

Steve remained in hospital for several days, content to remain in bed, being looked after by the nursing staff and spoilt by visits from Julie and his mum. He also had several interviews with DI Swift who surprisingly showed great concern over his welfare. During one of her visits she updated him on the police progress on the stolen vehicle criminal gang, telling him that Ray Tunes was now trying to save his own skin by giving information that had led to over a dozen arrest throughout the country.

Worrying for Steve was the fact that Carl Collins was still at large. Released from hospital, at home at last, he tried to put behind him thoughts of the terrible time he had been in incarcerated in that garage pit. Counselling had been offered to him but he was just happy to be home and in the care of his family, and of course Julie. The next weeks passed quickly his stitches were removed from his shoulder and he began to regain his fitness. It was time to think about his future. What better way to gather his thoughts than to go fishing. He went to the garden shed, and sure enough the old fishing poles that he and his brother once used were there in a corner. Removing one he saw there was still a line and hook attached. He tested the line, strong enough and the hook although rusty would do the job. He found a small flower pot and in the garden lifted a few old slabs to find several small worms. With them in the flower pot and the fishing pole over his shoulder, he called out to his mum to tell her where he was off to. He marched across the field to the bridge. Settling himself down he was able to fit his legs between the slats. Baiting the hook with a worm he pushed the pole between the slats and dangled the hook into the water, the same way he and his brother fished so many years ago. The weather was fine and, with the sun shining on his back, he placed his arms on the rail above his brother's plaque and lowered his head onto his arms feeling very contented, not caring if he caught a fish or not.

Steve was unaware of how long he remained in this position, but when his arms began to ache, he stood up to stretch his body. It was then he saw a figure approaching the bridge from the direction of his home. Wearing a black track suit with a hood partly obscuring the face the figure stopped at the side of the bridge, and Steve saw it was Carl Collins.

"I knew if I waited long enough I would find you alone," said Carl. "You have cost me everything, and now I am going to make you pay." He produced a long-bladed knife and, holding it in front of him, he stepped onto the bridge and moved towards Steve. "I would have finished you last time if that fucking knife hadn't broken. This one will do a better job." He lunged forward swinging the knife from side to side. Steve stepped back, not taking his eyes off the knife, and as he did so he stepped onto his fishing pole which rolled under his foot causing him to lose balance so he fell onto his back. Seeing his chance Carl leapt forward, dropping to his knees, straddling Steve's thighs.

He raised the knife above his head ready to drive it down into Steve's body, and as he did so the was a loud shout. "That's him!" Carl was distracted for a second, and Steve took his chance. Using the only weapon he had, he raised himself up and bent forward, smashing his head into Carl's chest. The impact caused Carl to fall backwards and the knife went spinning over his head to land with a thump behind him on the bridge floor. Both men got to their feet. Carl turned round and bent down to retrieve his knife, and without any hesitation, Steve moved forward and slammed his foot into Carl's backside, sending him sprawling forward. There was an agonising scream. Carl turned over, the knife protruding from the centre of his stomach.

Steve stood aghast at what he was seeing, then before he could react several police officers arrived at the scene. Carl was taken to hospital, and Steve who was uninjured was taken to the police station. Later, after giving a statement as to what had happened on the bridge he was allowed home. His mum then told him of how she saw a man she recognised as Carl Collins, get out of a car opposite her home as she was leaving to go shopping. She went back inside and dialled 999. Fortunately a police unit was already in Sweetwater dealing with another incident and was diverted to her home where she pointed out to them what was happening on the bridge.

Carl Collins was in a critical condition but doctors were hopeful he would survive. Although the police had witnessed the tragedy on the bridge, confirming that Carl's injury was a complete accident, Steve still felt responsible for Carl's injury. He made several attempts to find the police officer who had shouted out "That's him!" which had distracted Carl and undoubtedly saved his life, but both officers who had arrived first, denied calling out or hearing any such thing. Steve thought, did he just dream he heard those words or maybe he had had a flashback to the nightmares he had been having since he had been imprisoned. Whatever the mystery, something had made Carl hesitate from stabbing him and gave him the chance to use his head as a battering ram and knock him to the ground.

CHAPTER 13

Several weeks later Carl was released from hospital, taken into custody and charged with two attempts of murder and further offences involving handing stolen goods. During this time DI Swift contacted Steve with the news that forensics had identified the knife removed from Carl's stomach as the same knife used on both Jackie and Donna. This evidence was enough to question Carl about the murder of the two girls but he denied any knowledge of the girls' murders, saying he had found the knife in the boot of a car taken as part exchange for a new BMW at the showroom. They then had a breakthrough. A police diving unit training in a disused quarry outside Kelton found a Mercedes vehicle which was fitted with very distinguished spoked wheels. The vehicle was recovered and identified as the vehicle reported stolen from Collins just after Jackie's murder. A detective was sent to France with pictures of the Mercedes and the witness, Louise Hallet, positively identified it as the vehicle which nearly ran her over outside The Raven. Armed with this information, Carl was going to be interviewed further but, as DI Swift told Steve, so far all their evidence was circumstantial.

Carl was remanded in custody and sent to the prison to await trial on the charges brought against him. He was visited many times by Malcolm, but after several of these visits Malcolm appeared back at work in a distressed state. Julie noticed this and it soon became apparent that Steve had been right when he had suggested that there was more to Carl and Malcolm's relationship than just business partners. Julie felt compelled to offer her support to Malcolm, who broke down admitting that he and her brother had been lovers for a very long time, but now Carl had found someone else whilst in prison and did not want to see him ever again.

Hearing this from Julie, Steve contacted DI Swift and passed on the information. Malcolm was interviewed by DI Swift and he admitted that on the night Jackie had been murdered, he and Carl had one of their massive rows which resulted in Carl storming off and not returning until the early hours of the following morning. He remembered Carl was in a very dishevelled state, throwing his clothes into an old bag, and later that day he saw Carl burning the bag in a bin at the back of the showroom. He also remembered that Carl was at that time driving a Mercedes vehicle with very striking set of wheels. DI Swift asked him if he could tell her anything about the girl, Donna. Malcolm, in tears, said it was something he was trying to forget. Donna had caught him and Carl in a compromising position. Carl had sacked her the following day and she then disappeared. Carl had then told him not to worry about what Donna had seen, as she wouldn't bother them again.

CHAPTER 14

Steve was by this time getting frustrated with the police because after consultation with the CPS, they still did not, in their opinion, have the evidence to secure a conviction for at least Jackie's murder, and once and for all to clear his own name. Steve and Julie attended the court when Carl appeared to enter a plea to his charges. Leaving the court they were approached by a man Steve recognised from his time in prison as one of the prisoners who had been brutally picked on by prison officers. "You probably don't remember me," said the man, "But I have been following the stories in the press linked to you. I know how you stood up for me and the others when you were in prison. I was released only two days ago but for the past few weeks when in prison, I had a relationship with a man called Carl Collins, who I know is a killer."

"How the hell do you know that?" asked Steve.

The man replied, "Because he is so sure of himself that he confessed to me, saying the police haven't a clue about how he had murdered two girls who had called him a queer."

"Would you be willing to stand up in court and give that in evidence?" asked Steve.

"For what you did for us, yes I will, but the court might not believe me."

"Let's worry about that later," replied Steve, and as he did so he saw DI Swift leaving the court and shouted to her to come over. The man gave his name and details to DI Swift, and then repeated what he had just told Steve.

"This is crucial evidence, and it will be interesting to hear what Carl has to say when we interview him," said the DI, with a smile on her face. "I think the CPS will give the go ahead to charge him with the murder of Jackie and Donna whatever he comes up with."

Steve was at home, when the following week he had a call from DI Swift. "You are the first to know, but presented with all the evidence, Carl Collins has confessed to the murders of Jackie and Donna. He will be spending the rest of his life behind bars."

Steve phoned Julie with the news, trying not to be too exuberant, but she was so pleased that finally his name had been cleared and they could now put the past behind them and look to the future. Julie's father then came on the phone. He asked Steve if he had any plans for his future, telling him of his plans to buy Tunes garage, and would he be interested in taking on the management. Steve said he would give it some thought, but deep down he was pretty sure he could never forget his ordeal there. Steve also heard from his old Sergeant Bass and his long term friend John, who were in the process of opening a specialist centre for disabled forces personnel. They asked if he would be interested in joining them.

Then there was his old unfinished manuscript that was gathering dust in his bedroom since his release from prison, something he would love to complete.

Julie, who had now taken over the running of Collin Cars, told him she would support his decision whatever he decided to do. Yes, he decided, I am going to finish that story I started to write in prison, and if it's successful I will become a full time author for I have lots of material with my time in prison, the war in Afghanistan or even an autobiography.

CHAPTER 15

Steve recalled how the last few years had flown by. During this period he had become a very successful author and had written several best sellers, but now as he looked at the screen not having written a word for over twenty minutes, his mind was a blank. He glanced across the room to his beautiful wife breast-feeding their three-week-old daughter. His eyes fell to the play pen on the floor at her feet containing their two-year-old twin boys busy playing with building blocks. Sitting cross legged on the ground beside them was James, now a part of the family since his adoption had been completed. "Writers block," his wife said, smiling.

"Yes. Not sure how to end my autobiography, several thoughts, but hang on, you've just given me an idea." He looked back at the screen and began to type. I have to finish this story about my life and love, and can think of no better way than to write how lucky I am as I look across the room at my beautiful wife Julie, breast-feeding our three-week-old daughter. At her feet is a play pen containing our two-year-old twin boys busy playing with small wooden building bricks being carefully watched over by our adopted son James.

Contents

Printed in Great Britain
by Amazon

35820156R00057